DEAR MOUSE FRIENDS, WELCOME TO THE

STONE AGE!

Welcome to the Stone Age . . . and the World of the Cavemice!

Capital: Old Mouse City

Population: We're not sure. (Math doesn't exist yet!) But besides cavemice, there are plenty of dinosaurs, <u>way</u> too many saber-toothed tigers, and ferocious cave bears — but no mouse has ever had the courage to count them!

Typical Food: Petrified cheese soup

National Holiday: Great Zap Day, which celebrates the discovery of fire. Rodents exchange grilled cheese sandwiches on this holiday.

National Drink: Mammoth milkshakes

Climate: Unpredictable, with frequent meteor showers

cheese soup

milkshake

Money

Seashells of all shapes and sizes

Measurement

The basic unit of measurement is based on the length of the tail of the leader of the village. A unit can be divided into a half tail or quarter tail. The leader is always ready to present his tail when there is a dispute.

THE CAVEMICE

Geronimo

Trap

Thea

Benjamin

Bugsy Wugsy

Hercule Poirat

Grandma Ratrock

Geronimo Stilton

CAVEMICE

HELP, I'M IN HOT LAVA!

Scholastic Inc.

ISBN 978-0-545-64290-3

Copyright © 2011 by Edizioni Piemme S.p.A., Corso Como 15, 20154 Milan, Italy.

International Rights © Atlantyca S.p.A.

English translation © 2013 by Atlantyca S.p.A.

Based on an original idea by Elisabetta Dami.

www.geronimostilton.com

Published by Scholastic Inc., 557 Broadway, New York, NY 10012.
SCHOLASTIC and associated logos are trademarks and/or registered trademarks of Scholastic Inc.

Stilton is the name of a famous English cheese. It is a registered trademark of the Stilton Cheese Makers' Association. For more information, go to www.stiltoncheese.com.

Text by Geronimo Stilton
Original title *Sei nella lava fino al collo, Stiltonùt!*
Cover by Flavio Ferron
Illustrations by Giuseppe Facciotto (design) and Daniele Verzini (color)
Graphics by Marta Lorini

Special thanks to AnnMarie Anderson
Translated by Emily Clement
Interior design by Becky James

12 11 10 9 8 7 6 5 4 3   14 15 16 17 18/0

Printed in the U.S.A.   40
First printing, November 2013

MANY AGES AGO, ON PREHISTORIC MOUSE ISLAND, THERE WAS A VILLAGE CALLED OLD MOUSE CITY. IT WAS INHABITED BY BRAVE *RODENT SAPIENS* KNOWN AS THE CAVEMICE.

DANGERS SURROUNDED THE MICE AT EVERY TURN: EARTHQUAKES, METEOR SHOWERS, FEROCIOUS DINOSAURS, AND FIERCE GANGS OF SABER-TOOTHED TIGERS. BUT THE BRAVE CAVEMICE FACED IT ALL WITH A SENSE OF HUMOR, AND WERE ALWAYS READY TO LEND A HAND TO OTHERS.

HOW DO I KNOW THIS? I DISCOVERED AN ANCIENT BOOK WRITTEN BY MY ANCESTOR, GERONIMO STILTONOOT! HE CARVED HIS STORIES INTO STONE TABLETS AND ILLUSTRATED THEM WITH HIS ETCHINGS.

I AM PROUD TO SHARE THESE STONE AGE STORIES WITH YOU. THE EXCITING ADVENTURES OF THE CAVEMICE WILL MAKE YOUR FUR STAND ON END, AND THE JOKES WILL TICKLE YOUR WHISKERS! HAPPY READING!

Geronimo Stilton

WARNING! DON'T IMITATE THE CAVEMICE. WE'RE NOT IN THE STONE AGE ANYMORE!

AH, WHAT A FABUMOUSE DAY!

I woke up one Monday morning feeling bright-eyed and bushy-tailed. I gobbled down a slice of petrified cheddar quiche with a side of blueberries for breakfast.

YUMMY!

Then I chiseled a few tablets of notes for two articles that I would chisel later for *The Stone Gazette*.

Bones and stones! I forgot to introduce myself. I'm Geronimo Stiltonoot, and I'm a cavemouse. I run the most famous (well, the only) PREHISTORIC newspaper in Old Mouse City! (Actually, it's a stone slab. Paper hasn't been invented yet!)

I left my cave and headed toward my office at *The Stone Gazette*. It was a beautiful morning: The sky was clear and the sun was shining. There were no meteor showers in the forecast, and I didn't feel the tremor of a single EARTHQUAKE!

Ah, what a fabumouse day!

As I walked down the street, the rodents of *Old Mouse City* greeted me with happy **smiles** and **waves**.

When I arrived at the office, my coworkers were all working **peacefully**. I thought to myself once again:

Ah, what a fabumouse day!

At my desk, I had a burst of inspiration. I started to **CHISEL** busily, working on my article. Midway through the morning, I took a mammoth milkshake break. **YUMMY!**

Ah, what a fabu—

But before I could even finish the thought, **DISASTER** struck. A cat-astrophe had interrupted my peaceful morning!

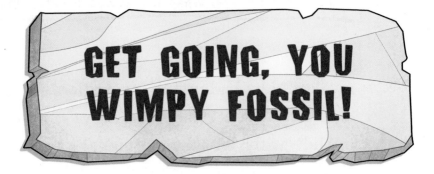

GET GOING, YOU WIMPY FOSSIL!

A **TORNADO** whirled into my office, kicking up a huge cloud of **dust** that ruined my mammoth milkshake. I was so startled, the **TABLET** I had been chiseling flew out of my paws and **shattered** against the desk, my hammer and chisel dropped to the ground, and my noise-canceling **earmuffs** went flying into the air.

It was a real **DISASTER**!

I was so scared, I couldn't move a muscle. I was **trembling** down to the tips of my **WHISKERS**!

Suddenly, I heard a familiar and very **bossy** voice.

"ON YOUR FEET, YOU WIMPY FOSSIL!" the voice squeaked. "What do you think you're doing? Catching a little **ratnap**? You're a real lazybones!"

I jumped in surprise. Me, a lazybones?! I'm **GERONIMO STILTONOOT**, the publisher of *The Stone Gazette*! I work all day, every day! And when I'm not working, I'm *thinking* about work! And when I'm *sleeping*, I'm *DREAMING* about work!

As soon as the cloud of dust cleared, the **massive, towering** shape of an elderly cavemouse with gray fur piled on top of her head and a huge club in her hands appeared. There was no doubt about it: It was **GRANDMA RATROCK**, the most stubborn, tough, and energetic rodent in prehistory!

I wasn't just dealing with a tornado. . . .

GRANDMA RATROCK

WHO SHE IS: GERONIMO'S GRANDMA

OCCUPATION: GIVING EVERYONE HER ADVICE AND OPINIONS, WHICH SOUND MORE LIKE ORDERS!

PERSONALITY: STUBBORN, TOUGH AS FOSSILIZED FETA, AND FULL OF ENERGY.

HOBBIES: SHE LOVES GOING ON DANGEROUS ADVENTURES, AND SHE ALWAYS TRIES TO DRAG ALONG HER GRANDSON.

HER FAVORITE PHRASE: "YOU ONLY LIVE ONCE, SO ALWAYS BE PREPARED FOR ADVENTURE!"

HER SECRET: ROMANTIC STORIES MAKE HER CRY.

This was much, much worse!

"**COME ON, GET OFF YOUR TAIL!**" she continued with the determination of a T. rex.

"But I — I —"

"I've told you a thousand times that a **TRUE JOURNALIST** must experience adventure before he writes about it!"

"But I — I —"

"How can you **CHISEL HISTORY** into stone if you haven't helped *make history*?"

"But I — I —"

"But nothing," Grandma scoffed. "Now, you come with me. I'm going to get you out of this **DUSTY** cave of an office and out into the prehistoric world! You'll have an adventure that mice will still be talking about MILLIONS OF YEARS from now!"

"Grandma Ratrock is right!"

1 jumped. My sister, Thea, had appeared out of nowhere. OH NO! She was always on our grandma's side.

Thea assumed the same stern expression as Grandma Ratrock.

You need action!

"You need action, Geronimo!" she exclaimed. "You need to put down that chisel for a while and experience some EXCITEMENT, thrills, and DANGER!"

Grandma Ratrock gloated with satisfaction.

"Listen to your sister,

11

Geronimo!" Grandma ordered.

"She's a smart rodent!"

I collapsed onto my rocky stool and **sighed**.

Petrified provolone! It was two against one, and I could tell I wasn't going to win this battle.

Petrified provolone!

YOU CAN'T MAKE ME!

Who knew what Grandma Ratrock had planned! Maybe it was a **DANGEROUS** mission to the lair of the ferocious  **TIGER KHAN** and his tribe of saber-toothed **TIGERS**. They were the number one enemy of the cavemice of Old Mouse City.

Or maybe it was a mission through hazards large and small to the *mysterious* Cave of Memories! Or maybe we'd face the terrifically terrifying —

"Listen to me, YOU FOSSILIZED RODENT!" my grandma scolded. "Stop daydreaming! Time is passing, and I'm not as YOUNG and strong as I once was —"

"But, Grandma," I interrupted her. "You're the most fit and in-shape rodent in all of *Old Mouse City*!"

"Yes, yes, I know," Grandma Ratrock agreed with a smile. "But you should have seen me when I was young! I could easily BEAT DOWN a cave bear! Ah, the good old days. . . ."

Grandma Ratrock rubbed

CAVE BEAR

14

her back with a pained expression. "But age catches up with us all, I'm afraid," she continued dramatically. "In fact, I've been suffering from some **Annoying** pains in my bones for some time now. Our shaman, **BLUSTER CONJURAT**, says that they're aging pains called **arthritis**."

"But, Grandma, you're the picture of health!" I insisted, trying to be kind. She really was in the best shape. "You never let anything slow you down —"

"SILENCE, HEARTLESS GRANDCHILD!" Grandma Ratrock squeaked.

"Don't make fun of a poor old rodent who's weak and wasting away like me!"

Weak and wasting away?! Grandma Ratrock was stronger and livelier than ten cavemice put together!

"As I was saying, these pains are very Annoying," Grandma continued. "And no one knows how to cure them!"

"Really?" I asked her, worried.

"Well, Bluster told me about a lost valley called *Cheesy~La*. According to legend, it's a paradise! The ancient inhabitants of Old Mouse City who suffered from aches and pains went there to be cured."

"But the land of *Cheesy~La* doesn't exist!" I replied. "It's mentioned in the *legends* of Old Mouse City, but no one has ever been there!"

Grandma Ratrock came up to my desk and **shook** her finger right under my snout.

"What have I **ALWAYS** told you, Grandson?" she shouted. "Legends are based on **truth**! So I want the whole Stiltonoot family to come with me in search of the land of *Cheesy~La*!"

Thea's face lit up and she clapped her paws.

"A mission to **discover** the lost land of Cheesy-La!" she squeaked. "I can't wait to get started!"

Petrified provolone! How could I make them understand what a **terrible** idea this was?

"But Cheesy-La isn't **REAL**!" I insisted. "It's just a fantasy land. It's the stuff of myths and legends! No one's ever been there, and there's no **map** to show us how to get there! I won't do it!

I'M NOT BUDGING!
I'M NOT GOING!
YOU CAN'T MAKE ME!"

THE VOLCANO IS THE WAY!

I was determined. I wasn't going to let Grandma Ratrock and Thea convince me to go on a quest to find a mythical place no one had ever been to! No way, no how!

"Unnnnncle!" a happy voice squeaked. "Hooray! We're going to Cheesy-La!"

I jumped. It was my dear nephew Benjamin! I was SURPRISED to see him there.

He was at the door to my office, and my cousin Trap was right behind him. Finally, the shaman, Bluster, and his daughter, Clarissa Conjurat, filed in. Ah, Clarissa was the most CHARMING rodent in Old Mouse City! I was head over tail for her!

It was as if the whole village was at a meeting in my office. Soon there would be more people around my desk than in **Singing Rock Square** at rush hour!

"Don't be such a wimp, Cuz!" Trap started in on me. "You have the chance to get some fresh air, but you want to stay here with your boring, cold stone tablets! Follow my lead: I've closed the **Rotten Tooth Tavern** for a few days and I'm going to make this trip into a real **VACATION!**"

I opened my mouth to reply, but —

"Trap is right, Uncle!" Benjamin chirped enthusiastically. "We'll have so much **FUN** together! Come on! Pretty please with **cheese** on top?"

Everyone was *ignoring* a very important fact.

21

"I'm telling you, *Cheesy~La* does not **exist**!" I squeaked loudly.

"That is **NOT** true," Bluster replied suddenly, startling me. "I have proof Cheesy-La exists. **Look!**"

He tossed me a very **HEAVY** stone tablet. Unfortunately, I wasn't expecting it, and it landed right on my paw! **Ouchie!**

Ouchie, ouchie, ouchie!

I rubbed my poor, **sore** paw. The pain **distracted** me for a moment — that is, until Grandma Ratrock **pinched** my tail.

"Come on, Grandson!" she squeaked. "We don't have geological eras to waste! Tell us what's on the **tablet**!"

I picked up the stone: It seemed very **old**. **"This tablet came from the Cave of Memories**," Bluster explained solemnly.

I was surprised: The Cave of Memories was the place where all the **stories** from our local history were kept! Was it possible that some pre-prehistoric mouse had really left traces of the **mysterious** land of Cheesy-La?

Bluster pointed to the **PICTURES** cut into the stone.

"This is *proof* of the existence of the legendary land of Cheesy-La!" the shaman declared confidently. "And the ancient ones even tell us how to get there!"

Everyone's eyes **widened** in amazement.

"OHHHHHHH!"

"Look here," Bluster continued. "This design tells us we must go to the **Cheddar Volcano** to find the path to *Cheesy~La*!"

Great rocky
boulders, not
the Cheddar
Volcano!

Help!

Rivers of
molten lava
would **Singe**
my tail . . .

Pee-yew!

. . . I would suffocate
from deadly,
STINKY fumes . . .

Ouch!

. . . and I would
be crushed in an
avalanche of volcanic
ROCKS!

"But I don't want to lose my tail in a volcanic EXPLOSION!" I protested.

"EXCUSES, EXCUSES!" Bluster scolded me. "You're steps away from discovering the truth and you want to give up before you've even begun?"

I was about to argue when I realized that Clarissa (**oh, what a lovely rodent!**) was looking at me with her stone-gray eyes.

Clarissa, the loveliest rodent in all of Old Mouse City!

YOU'LL BE A HERO!

Staring at Clarissa made me tongue-tied. She's such an intelligent, **marvemouse** rodent!

"You really don't want to go on the trip, Geronimo?" Clarissa asked sweetly.

Just hearing her squeak had a strange effect on me. My heart was HAMMERING in my ears, and my legs felt weak, as if they were made of melted cheese!

"You'd really **REFUSE** to help find a cure for your dear grandma's aches and pains?" Clarissa continued.

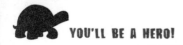

"The discovery of Cheesy-La wouldn't just help Grandma Ratrock — you would be **helping** so many other ailing rodents in Old Mouse City as well. You'll be a **HERO**!"

Suddenly, I had a vision of a **CROWD** of mice carrying me in the AiR.

For a moment, I imagined **Ernest Heftymouse**, the village chief, crushing (I mean, shaking) my paw with pride while Clarissa smiled at me.

"Well, okay!" I agreed. "Let's do it!"

"YESSSSSS!"

Benjamin squeaked, jumping up to **hug** me.

Thea and Trap exchanged a satisfied look.

"Oh, I hope we get to see a volcanic **ERUPTION**!" Benjamin said excitedly. "And maybe we'll spot a real live **T. REX** in the wild! I've never seen one before."

I turned as **pale** as a piece of **fossilized feta**. I had a moment of panic.

WHAT HAD I AGREED TO?!

Everyone was so busy chattering about

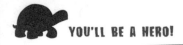

the adventure, I thought maybe I could slip out of my office and hide somewhere until the expedition left without me.

Just as I was about to *dash* out the door, Grandma Ratrock grabbed me by the collar and **DRAGGED** me back inside.

There's no time to waste!

"Oh no, you don't!" she scolded me. "Now let's get moving. There's no time to **WASTE**! We have an **expedition** to prepare for!"

ONLY AN HOUR IN . . .

Grandma Ratrock marched me straight home to my cave, where she began *racing* around, grabbing clubs, food, and blankets to take with us.

"We'll need some nice **meat** and a few wheels of **cheese**," she said as she **STUFFED** the items into a green sack. "Then we'll need a **WOODEN** club because you never know, a dinosaur **BONE** club because you never know, a **STONE** club because you never know, and a **torch** — because you never know! Oh, look! You even made your grandma's favorite cheesy moss **SOUP**! We'll take that, too!"

Bones and stones! Weak and wasting away? Grandma Ratrock was ZIPPING around my cave faster than I could!

As soon as we were packed, Grandma and I met up with Thea, Trap, and Benjamin. Grandma Ratrock set the (INCREDIBLY FAST!) pace as we crossed Old Mouse City and arrived at the edge of the village. Evidently, Grandma had forgotten all about her TERRIBLE aches, because we made it there in RECORD time!

HOLEY CHEESE, WE WERE ONLY AN HOUR IN AND I WAS ALREADY EXHAUSTED!

Meanwhile, all the others seemed as fresh as ferns. We arrived at the WALL that surrounded the village. My whiskers began to tremble in fear as we went through the gate.

BAM! The gate slammed shut, and we were all alone on the EMPTY plateau that towered over Old Mouse City. The terrifying Cheddar Volcano loomed in the distance.

GULP!

Huff ... puff ... puff!

Yahoo!

Any courage I had **evaporated** like a puff of smoke from a **fiery** volcano!

Thea **pointed** to the volcano with excitement.

"LOOK OVER THERE!" she exclaimed. "WHAT A SIGHT!"

Grandma Ratrock nodded in agreement. "And we've made it this far so quickly," she said. "I don't feel tired at all!"

"And smell that fresh air!" Trap said, breathing in deeply.

My eyes widened: Fresh air?! The valley air surrounding Cheddar Volcano actually had a terribly **STINKY** odor!

Clusters of smelly clouds fluttered here and there. The **STENCH** was worse than the odor of the most pungent gorgonzola! UGH!

Suddenly, I thought I saw a **shadow**

pass by out of the corner of my eye . . . but maybe it was just my overactive imagination.

"**COME ON, LET'S GO!**" Thea urged me impatiently. "What are we waiting for?"

Ah, what fresh air!

I was so exhausted, and I really needed a rest. But I didn't dare complain. I was afraid Grandma Ratrock would give my tail another PINCH!

"COME ON!" Grandma ordered us. "We must make our way around the volcano and find a path or a sign that points us in the direction of Cheesy-La!"

Then her face lit up and she placed her paw on my shoulder. "From this point on, YOU will lead the way, Grandson!"

Petrified provolone! Why did I have to lead the way?!

"But why me, Grandma?" I asked, still gasping for breath.

"Because you're the SLOWEST of all of us!" she replied. "Did I say the SLOWEST? You're also the most scared! Did I say the most scared? You're also the —"

"Okay, okay," I interrupted. "That's enough, I get it!"

I started to walk in front of everyone, on the **scariest** path I had ever taken in my life. The sun was beating down on us so strongly that it felt like I was walking on **Hot coals**!

A few steps later, I again thought I saw a **shadow** just behind us. I also had the strange sensation that we were being **watched**! Could someone (or something — *yikes!*) be following us?

I used my paw to shield my eyes from the **blinding** sun. I looked to the **right**. Nothing! I looked to the **left**. Nothing! I looked **UP**. Nothing! I looked **down**. Nothing!

But I was really, really **worried**. The Cheddar Volcano was right between Old

Mouse City and the camp of Tiger Khan's ferocious SABER-TOOTHED SQUAD! What if a saber-toothed tiger had noticed us?

I was about to warn the others about my suspicion when I placed a **paw** on a pile of fresh ferns. Suddenly, the ground gave way under my paws!

AHHHHHHHHHHHHHH!

I fell right into an underground tunnel!

TRULY TRAPPED!

Once I had recovered from my fall, I looked around me, bewildered.

"Uncle Geronimo!" little Benjamin shouted from the top of the hole. "Can you hear me?"

"ARE YOU ALL RIGHT, GRANDSON?" Grandma Ratrock added.

"Y-yes . . . I-I'm okay!" I replied. "I ONLY hurt my paws, my back, my tail, my snout, and my whiskers!"

"We'll get you out of there!" Thea said **reassuringly**.

But then I looked around myself.

"No, don't do that!" I replied. "You should all **come down** here instead!"

"Are you joking?" Trap asked, confused. I heard him whispering to the others, "He must have **HIT** his head."

But I wasn't joking. I had just noticed a very interesting boulder. It was a truly amazing discovery!

"What we're looking for is right down here!" I announced

Come down here!

triumphantly. "It's a sign **pointing** out the way to Cheesy-La!"

As soon as I said the word *Cheesy-La*, Grandma Ratrock suddenly exploded in a prehistoric yell.

"**DID YOU HEAR THAT?**" she shrieked. "Get moving! Everyone down there with Geronimo!"

I heard what sounded like an approaching avalanche. **RRRRUUUMBLE!**

A moment later, Grandma Ratrock came **tumbling** down in a

shower of rocks and landed right on my head.

OUCH! WHat a PreHistoric Pain iN tHe NecK!

Thea, Trap, and little Benjamin came tumbling down after Grandma, creating another shower of **pebbles** and **STONES**.

"Show us what you found, Geronimo!" Grandma Ratrock demanded.

I pointed to the large **BOULDER** that I had spotted earlier.

Carved into the stone was a picture of a mysterious pool of water with enormouse **bubbles** coming out of it. It was the same **PiCTURE** that we had seen on Bluster Conjurat's tablet!

Thea studied the art closely.

"The carving clearly says that the way to *Cheesy~La* is behind this boulder!"

Thea announced dramatically. "Come on, everyone. We have to PUSH this boulder aside!"

HEAVE-HO! HEAVE-HO!

We pushed as hard as we could, but nothing happened. The boulder didn't move an inch! We were sweating through

our fur! We pushed and pushed, again and again. Finally, after the HUNDREDTH try, the colossal boulder moved just enough to let us pass through.

The narrow passageway opened into a deep tunnel that led **DOWN**, **DOWN**, **DOWN**, below the Cheddar Volcano.

All around us it was **DARK** and gloomy, but the path was next to a small stream of **molten lava** that lit our way. The lava didn't just give off light, though — it also created so much heat that it **singed** our tails! And as if that wasn't enough, the tunnel was so long it seemed it would never end!

"Get a move on!" Grandma scolded us. "We've got company. I noticed some TIGER PAW PRINTS in the dirt just before we went down that mouse hole."

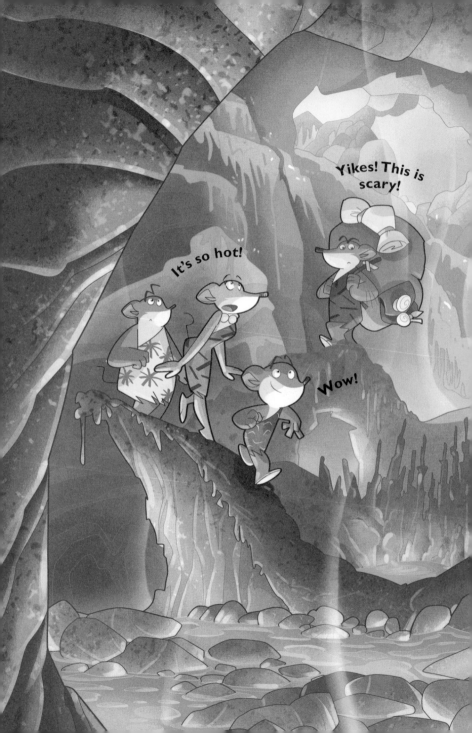

So it was **true**! We were being followed by some saber-toothed tigers!

Between the **boiling** molten lava of the volcano and the **FANGED** felines who couldn't wait to make a delicious **mouse-meat** meal out of us, we were TRULY TRAPPED!

Yummy... mouse meat!

A RIVER OF BOILING LAVA!

As our descent under the volcano continued, the STReam of lava that ran alongside our path through the tunnel started to get **bigger** and **bigger**. Soon it had turned into a gigantic river of boiling lava!

It was so hot, my whiskers were singed off!

Suddenly, we were forced to stop.

The river of **lava**, which to that point had calmly flowed alongside us, now curved sharply and blocked our path! We were stuck!

The only way forward was to cross over the **enormouse** expanse of *burning-hot* magma. But how would we do it?

"Hey!" Benjamin exclaimed, pointing above us. "Look at all the **roots**!"

It was true: Countless **THICK** and **knotted** roots from the trees on the surface above us hung like vines from the rocky ceiling of the tunnel.

"Grandma, are you **thinking** what I'm thinking?" Thea asked.

Grandma's eyes twinkled with excitement. "**OH NO!**" I moaned, guessing their risky plan. They were planning to grab the roots and swing across the lava! If we fell in, we would all be **mouse fondue**!

Bones and stones! Why had I agreed to come on this trip?

"Stop **complaining** and follow us, Geronimo!" Grandma ordered me.

She took an athletic jump and grabbed one of the roots, **swinging** toward another root. Then she grasped the second root with her other paw and continued to move forward, root by root, just as if they were **vines**! She managed to cross the river of **boiling** lava easily.

FOSSILIZED FETA, what an acr⊙bat! Weak and wasting away? It didn't look that way to me!

Wheeeeee!

Once Grandma Ratrock made it across, she urged the rest of us to follow.

Thea didn't have to be told twice — she FLEW from root to root like Mousezan, reaching the other side in a flash.

Then it was Trap's turn. He carried BENJAMIN on his back and followed Grandma's and Thea's examples.

I was as PALE as mozzarella with worry, but little Benjamin looked like he was having the time of his life as he dangled over the HOT lava.

Way to go!

Once he and Trap had landed safely on the other side, I was the only one left.

"Come on, Cuz!" Trap called out. "What are you still doing over there?"

I had been **FOSSILIZED** with fear — I couldn't move a single singed whisker!

Thea lost her patience.

"Make up your mind, Geronimo!" she squeaked. "Either cross the river of lava, or you'll end up in the jaws of the **SABER-TOOTHED SQUAD**!"

"Yeah!" Trap agreed. "What's it going to be, Geronimo? The lava or the tigers? Huh? Huh? Huh?"

"Don't pressure me!" I squeaked back. But Thea's threat had worked. I tried to control my trembling paws as I slowly moved forward and grabbed the first root.

I must not look down! I must not look down! I thought to myself as I reached for the second root, and the third. But, at the fourth root, I glanced below me. I was dangling right over the middle of the river of lava! I had never been so close to extinction before!

I lost my **concentration** and grabbed the next root while I was too **low**. The burning lava singed my tail.

YOOOUUUCH!

Out of panic, I **swung** forward, grabbed another root, and quickly launched myself toward the other side. As soon as I placed my poor **burned** paws on the rocks, I collapsed in a heap.

WHEW! I WAS SAFE!

SKREEEAAAK!
SKREEEAAAK!

Trap didn't let me rest for long.

"COME ON, COME ON," he urged, giving me a shake. "So you made it across the river of lava — big deal! This is no time to take a nap. Let's keep moving!"

We hurried on, leaving the lava behind us. Finally, the temperature began to drop and we were able to breathe some fresh air. **AHHHH!**

Grandma Ratrock marched ahead at full speed. Suddenly, she stopped in her tracks. It wasn't lava that stopped her this time. It was a true **GEOLOGICAL*** **WONDER**! We were standing in an enormouse cave full of hundreds of **STALACTITES** and **STALAGMITES**. The sight took my breath away!

Then a sharp, piercing sound startled us.

EEEEEEK! EEEEEEK!

A PREHISTORIC BAT swirled threateningly around our heads. It was small, but it had sharp fangs and claws! And it didn't seem at all happy that we had just entered its cave.

"Maybe it's just saying hello?" Trap suggested, scratching his head.

"I don't think so!" Benjamin replied nervously. "I've studied bats in school. They use that noise to call other bats!"

Unfortunately, Benjamin was right. A moment later, the cave was invaded by **hundreds** of **terrifying** bats with fangs. There were so many of them!

We flattened ourselves on the ground and

tried to protect each other, but the **Bats** headed right for us.

FOSSILIZED FETA! We were about to kiss our tails good-bye!

We were just **seconds** away from **extinction** when we heard a new sound. It was even louder and more terrifying than the sound of the **swarming** bats.

SKREEEAAAK!

The bats hovered in the air in fear and surprise.

Suddenly, the prehistoric bats seemed more afraid than we were! Before we were able to understand who or what had made that terrible noise, the

bats immediately **flew** away. We were saved!

But wait: What am I saying? If there was an even SCARIER beast in that cave than the prehistoric bats, then we were truly in trouble.

THINGS WERE GOING FROM BAD TO WORSE!

Suddenly, I felt someone grab me by the collar. It was Thea.

"GET UP, Geronimo!" she shouted. "Someone figured out how to get us out of this mess! Look!"

I raised my head, feeling hopeful.

In front of me was my cousin Trap.

He was holding his paws around his mouth. He was the one who had made that **terrifying** sound!

"That's the call of the famouse WHISKERED PTERODACTYL!" Trap explained triumphantly. "It's the prehistoric bat's greatest enemy!"

I couldn't believe it: We were saved!

"Thank you, thank you," Trap gloated, making a little bow. "I know . . . I'm a genius!"

I had to admit it: For once, he was RIGHT!

THE WHISKERED PTERODACTYL

The whiskered pterodactyl was a flying reptile. It had a strange handlebar mustache. It was a very picky prehistoric creature. In fact, it *only* ate prehistoric bats!

Handlebar mustache

Some scientists think the whiskered pterodactyl used its long, curly mustache like a lasso to catch unsuspecting bats. But other scientists have no idea what the mysterious mustache was for.

THE CRYSTAL LABYRINTH

Once the BATS had flown away, we made it through the cave of stalactites and stalagmites.

The **path** became straight again, but the dull gray cave walls began changing. Suddenly, they were covered in sparkling crystals!

As we passed close to the SHiMMERiNG walls, I noticed some of the crystals had deep scratches on them. I wondered why, but there was no time to stop and think about it. Grandma Ratrock and the others had disappeared from sight!

"Wait up!" I squeaked. "Wait for me!"

I hurried to catch up to the others. After a little while, the tunnel **branched off**, and the main path turned into parallel paths and corridors of various sizes. We tried to stay on what we thought was the main **PATH**, but we soon realized that we'd **LOST** our way!

We tried to retrace our steps to find a way out, but each time we went in one direction, we wound up **BACK** where we started. Or, at least, it seemed like that. . . . Those crystals all looked the **same**!

IT WAS A REAL LABYRINTH!

Benjamin squeezed my paw nervously.

To distract him, I showed him some **INSECT LARVAE** that had been trapped inside the crystals.

While we were studying the larvae, Benjamin noticed something.

"Look at this scratch on the crystal, Uncle!" he said.

"Oh, I'm sure that's just erosion," I replied.

"Look again, Uncle!" Benjamin insisted.

I peered at the crystal more closely and **SMACKED** my paw against my forehead. Why hadn't I realized it sooner?

"You're right, Benjamin!" I exclaimed. "This isn't a scratch — it's an **arrow**!"

We were **saved** once again!

We deciphered one sign after another. The scratches were arrows that gave us **directions** for how to get out of the **LABYRINTH**! Hopefully, our ancestors had scratched the way all the way to *Cheesy~La* for us!

WHAT A DISAPPOINTMENT!

To our great surprise, we exited the tunnel and **POPPED** up outside!

Everything was covered in what seemed to be a light fog.

"It's not fog, it's *STEAM*!" Thea said.

She was right. All around us, pools of hot water bubbled, letting off *puffs* of *STEAM*. There were small volcanoes everywhere, and the ground **RUMBLED** beneath our paws.

"Hmm," Grandma Ratrock mused. "Pools of bubbling water? Volcanoes everywhere? I think we've found the valley of *Cheesy-La*!"

Our tails drooped as we looked around us in **disappointment**. Could this really be the legendary land of Cheesy-La? *This* was **paradise**? Aside from the **steamy** volcanoes and the **boiling** pools of water, there was nothing there!

"Let's LOOK around," GRANDMA encouraged us. "Now that we've found Cheesy-La, we must find a cure for my aches!"

This is it?

...and steam!

It's just bubbles ...

So we explored the volcanic valley. We searched FAR and **wide**, HIGH and low, LEFT to RIGHT, and even FRONT to BACK. But we found nothing — absolutely nothing! There were just a lot of bubbles, boiling streams of lava, and **lots** and **lots** and **lots** of steam.

Cheesy-La was nothing but a remote, deserted valley, thousands and thousands of tail lengths away from Old Mouse City.

Ugh!

What a disappointment!

What a disappointment!

It looked like there was no cure for Grandma Ratrock's aches and pains. The paradise of Cheesy-La really did only exist in legends!

"On the plus side, at least the SABER-TOOTHED SQUAD didn't follow us here," I said with a sigh of relief.

With our tails between our legs, we turned around to make our way back to Old Mouse City.

STOP, ROTTEN RODENTS!

We began to retrace our pawsteps, heading back in the direction of Old Mouse City. Suddenly, we heard a growling voice from inside the **ROCKY TUNNEL** we had exited a few moments earlier.

"STOP WHERE YOU ARE, ROTTEN RODENTS!"

We were petrified. Only one creature growled like that. . . .

It was the most **POWERFUL** and **THREATENING** figure in the land! He emerged from the darkness of the tunnel —

it was **TIGER KHAN**!

The terrible, ferocious **saber-toothed** tiger was the **NUMBER ONE** enemy of the cavemice of Old Mouse City and the supreme **CHIEF** of the Saber-Toothed Squad!

The blood **chilled** in my veins at the sight of his long, **SHARP** fangs. Behind Tiger Khan, three other **TIGERS** stepped

forward and growled at us **menacingly**.
Fossilized Feta! We were in **big**
trouble. **REALLY BIG** trouble. We were in
the **BIGGEST** trouble possible!

Tiger Khan exploded in evil laughter. It
made my fur stand on end!

"**BWAHAHAHA!**" he cackled.
"You subspecies of fossilized rodents! You
didn't even realize two of my faithful felines
were following you!"

That wasn't true! Grandma Ratrock and I
had had a hunch. But I decided to keep my
snout shut.

"Are you looking for some kind of
TREASURE?" Tiger Khan asked. "I
knew there was something *mysterious*
about this valley of volcanoes! Come on,
hand over the *loot*. That treasure is
MINE!"

So that was why the felines had followed us but hadn't **attacked** yet! They thought we were searching for some kind of hidden TREASURE!

"*What treasure?*" Trap spluttered before we could stop him. "There's no treasure here, you lousy feline! Can't you see that there's nothing here but water and steam? The legend was wrong."

The tigers surrounded us and bared their SHARP fangs hungrily.

"WHAT?!" growled Tiger Khan. "No treasure? Well, we'll get something here — we'll gobble you up! We'll have minced mice for dinner!"

"Paws off, sewer breath!" Grandma Ratrock suddenly shouted. "GET OUT OF HERE, YOU FILTHY FELINES!"

We all turned to stare at Grandma Ratrock

in **shock**. Tiger Khan glared at her in disbelief.

"**HOW DARE YOU?!**" he roared. "For your arrogance, you'll be our first mouthful of the day!"

"Why, it would be my pleasure, you **snaggle-toothed** excuse for a **kitty cat**!" Grandma replied without batting an eye. "Now go scratch your **fleas** somewhere else: We have work to do here!"

Shoo, kitty!

THEA, Trap, Benjamin, and I were speechless. GRANDMA didn't seem to be afraid of the Saber-Toothed Squad at all!

Tiger Khan looked like he was about to EXPLODE with anger. Grandma's bravery had left him **speechless**. He had no idea how to reply!

"It was such a pain to get here," Grandma Ratrock continued. "I don't want any more hitches!"

Our gaze shifted from Grandma to Tiger Khan and back again. What was going to happen next?

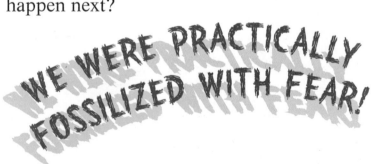

WE WERE PRACTICALLY FOSSILIZED WITH FEAR!

SEIZE THEM!

Once he got over his surprise, Tiger Khan took action.

"SEIZE THEM! TRAP THEM! CAGE THEM!"

he shouted to his faithful feline guards. "Fatten them up! I want to dine on MICE tonight!"

The tigers moved toward us, baring their sharp, shining FANGS.

Tiny beads of sweat were streaming down my fur. Grandma Ratrock, on the other hand, looked calm and peaceful. She stood there facing the ferocious felines

without twitching a whisker.

Just then, something incredible happened.

A strong spurt of **boiling** water erupted from the ground with a deafening gurgle, blasting into the air.

WHOOOSSSHHH!

The powerful jet of water knocked over the first tiger, then the second, the third, and the fourth. They were quickly blasted far, far away!

We ran for cover and ducked under some ROCKY BOULDERS to avoid the boiling blasts of water. In the course of a few minutes, the Saber-Toothed Squad had been completely SURPRISED and beaten back by the squirts of steamy water!

"AHHH! I HATE WATER!"

yowled one of the terrorized tigers.

"What's going on?" I asked my sister, Thea, **bewildered**.

"These spurts are called GEYSERS!" she explained. "They're

Help!

Run!

eruptions of hot water from underground caused by being near a volcano!"

The tigers continued to fly up into the air like kernels of **POPCORN** as the geyser blasts continued. The geysers had filled the air with clouds of **steam**, and we couldn't see a thing!

Suddenly, I had an idea.

"This is our chance to **ESCAPE**!" I shouted

Let's get out of here!

to Grandma, Thea, Trap, and Benjamin. "Come on! Follow me! Let's get out of here!"

I started RUNNING away from the tigers.

Tiger Khan realized that we were getting away and tried to follow us, **zigzagging** between the geysers, waving his club wildly.

Suddenly, I saw a **small gap** in the rocks: If we could squeeze in there, we would be saved! And with a bit of **luck**, Tiger Khan and the Saber-Toothed Squad wouldn't be able to follow us.

One by one, we **slipped** through the gap in the rocks and entered a dark, mysterious **CAVE**.

To keep from being discovered, we had to stay **very, very quiet**. . . .

ON YOUR FEET, YOU ROASTED FELINES!

We stayed **hidden** in the cave for what felt like forever. Finally, we heard the geysers stop spraying steam just as suddenly as they'd started. Peace and quiet returned to the valley of Cheesy-La.

I peeked out of the cave and saw the tigers lying on the ground, their tails singed by the **VIOLENT** jets of hot water and steam.

"On your feet, you roasted felines!" Tiger Khan ordered.

"FIND THOSE MICE AND BRING THEM TO ME!"

The members of the Saber-Toothed Squad got up and, **bruised** and **limping**, they began to search for us.

Suddenly, Tiger Khan looked in the direction of the cave where we were **hiding**! I slipped back into the shadows, gesturing

to the others to be very, very quiet.

My heart was pounding in my chest. **Ba-bump! Ba-bump! Ba-bump!**

I hugged my dear nephew Benjamin to protect him — and also to give myself some COURAGE!

Tiger Khan stuck his nose in the narrow opening, and a few of his WHiSKeRS almost touched my paw. I thought I might faint from fear. But the cave was **dark**, and Tiger Khan couldn't see us. He retreated, and a moment later, we heard him scolding the other members of the Saber-Toothed Squad.

"Those **rotten rodents** managed to escape!" he shouted. "Which one of you let them past you? HUH? HUH? HUH?"

We waited in the safety of our hiding place until we were sure the FEROCIOUS

TIGERS were gone. No one made a PEEP because we were all holding our breath. When it had been quiet outside the cave for a few minutes, Grandma Ratrock finally spoke up.

"THEY'RE GONE!" she announced loudly. "We're saved again!"

"Hooray!" Thea, Benjamin, and Trap cheered. I just sighed in relief.

I peeked out of the cave and saw that Grandma was right. The valley was deserted once again — there was no trace of the tigers anywhere. There was just steam, steam, and more steam!

THE SECRET OF CHEESY-LA

Tentatively, we ventured toward the entrance of the cave and prepared to step back out into the sunlight.

"Wait a minute!" Benjamin suddenly exclaimed. We stood just inside the mouth of the **cave**. "Look over there!"

Benjamin pointed to the rocky walls around us.

"What is it, Benjamin?" Thea asked him.

"Have you seen this WALL?" he asked us.

Now that our eyes were used to the darkness, we could see where Benjamin was pointing. We were shocked and AMAZED. The walls of the cave were completely covered in **PAINTINGS**. And they revealed the secret of *Cheesy-La*!

The pictures showed ancient pre-prehistoric cavemice in the **pools** of hot water. They were lounging around, looking very **happy** and *relaxed*.

Of course!

Those pools of bubbling water themselves were the treatment for **aching bones**! This was the famouse cure that the shaman, Buster Conjurat, had been talking about: Cheesy-La was a STONE AGE SPA!

From the pictures, we learned that the **mud** could be spread over the fur to relieve **aches** and **pains**. Breathing in the natural **steam** was good for the lungs, and *drinking* the hot, volcanic water helped cure tummy troubles!

Cheesy-La didn't look like much, but it really was a *paradise* for any mouse seeking a prehistoric health treatment. As much as I hated to admit it, GRANDMA RATROCK had been right.

SO MUCH FOR ACHES!

Grandma Ratrock **bolted** out of the cave as fast as a meteorite. She couldn't wait to try out this prehistoric treatment!

After a **walk** around to check out all of Cheesy-La, she stopped in front of a pool of **bubbling** water.

"This is fabumouse," she **squeaked** happily. "We're a nice distance from the **lava** and the **GEYSERS**!"

She leaned down and dipped her paw in the water.

"It's not too **HOT** and not too **COLD**," she announced. "It's the perfect **temperature**!"

She took a few steps back and suddenly ran forward, leaping into the pool of water. "INCOMING!" she shouted, landing in the water with an enormouse *splash*.

"**Way to Go!**" Benjamin cheered enthusiastically.

"Come on in!" Grandma told us. "This water feels **mouse-tastic**! My bones already feel a millennium younger!"

THEA hopped right in, and so did little **BENJAMIN**. When they were all in the water, they started to play, SPLASHING in the pool.

I looked around for Trap but didn't see him anywhere.

Hmmm, that's strange, I thought. He had just been there with us a minute ago.

I **inched** toward the side of the pool, trying to decide if I would get in.

Suddenly, there was a shout, and a **dark** shadow fell over me. A second later, a **HUGE** boulder knocked me to the ground.

I was being crushed!

Completely unable to move, I opened my eyes to find that the boulder was none other than my cousin **Trap**!

"Oh, thank goodness, Cuz!" Trap said with a sigh. "I leaped into the pool, but I had terrible

aim. If it hadn't been for you, I would have been **smashed** on the ground! You saved me."

"**Oh, No problem,**" I grumbled. "Now I'm the one who's smashed!"

Once Trap moved, I was finally able to get in the pool. My muscles were really aching since Trap had landed on top of me. But I have to say again that Grandma was right. That hot water was a real cure — I felt invigorated!

A little later, Grandma Ratrock came up and hugged me, taking me by surprise.

"I want to thank you for being a part of this **expedition**, Geronimo," she said, giving me an enormouse **thump** on the shoulder. It almost made me **crumple** in pain. **OUCHie!**

Still, I smiled. Even if Grandma's displays

of affection were a bit **ROUGH**, she meant well.

Thea, Trap, and Benjamin surrounded me and gave me a big hug as well.

"I'm so glad we're a family," Benjamin said sweetly. "We always have the best adventures!"

He was right. The Stiltonoot family may be a little strange, but we have a **fabumouse** time together!

HOORAY FOR THE STILTONOOTS!

Our return trip was **uneventful**. All the obstacles we'd faced on the journey to Cheesy-La didn't seem so DANGEROUS now. In fact, they seemed like *fun*!

After following the underground tunnel back out, we enjoyed the **FRESH** air as we hightailed it back to *Old Mouse City* in no time at all!

We were SURPRISED to find a large welcoming committee **greeting** us when we arrived.

The village chief, ERNEST HEFTYMOUSE, was waiting for us along with his wife, Chattina. Bluster Conjurat was by their side with his daughter, Clarissa (ah, what a lovely rodent), and all the inhabitants of Old Mouse City were right behind them.

They had been waiting for us for quite some time, **eager** to find out the result of our **expedition**!

"So, what do you have to tell us?" Ernest asked impatiently.

"This is a great day for Old Mouse City!"

Grandma said proudly. "We have found the lost land of Cheesy-La! It's a real STONE AGE SPA, and every mouse in Old Mouse City can enjoy it!"

The rodents of the village cheered loudly, applauding and shouting our names. It was just as I imagined.

Ernest proclaimed the Stiltonoot family the **discoverers** of Cheesy-La, and he invited

everyone to Singing Rock Square that night for a lavish banquet in our honor!

I had already started thinking of several articles that I would chisel in *The Stone Gazette* about all of the incredible adventures we'd had.

At the end of the welcoming celebration, we all headed home to prepare for the banquet. As I was walking home, a low, sweet voice called out to me.

"Geronimo!"

I knew that squeak! I turned and saw Clarissa's lovely gray eyes looking back at me.

Gulp! I was so nervous!

"Thank you for finding Cheesy~La," she told me. "You and your family are real heroes! Now all the ailing rodents

112

of Old Mouse City can finally cure their **aches** and **pains!**"

I felt myself **blush** to the tips of my whiskers. She had called me a **hero**! It was just as I had imagined.

"It . . . it was nothing, Clarissa. . . ." I stuttered. "It was p-practically a walk in the park!"

Clarissa smiled. "Well, I wanted to **THANK YOU** with a little gift," she said.

Then she presented me with a bottle of prehistoric perfume.

"No offense, Geronimo, but after your journey, your **FUR** could use some freshening," she said sweetly.

Great rocky boulders, how embarrassing! I must have smelled like a cavemouse from the sewer. It was **NOT** just as I had imagined!

"Th-Thank you, Clarissa," I stuttered, unsure of what to say.

"You're welcome!" she squeaked, and she leaned over and gave me a tiny peck on the snout.

My legs turned to melted cheese. I felt like the **happiest** mouse in prehistory!

Here in the Stone Age, life might be tougher than fossilized feta, but there were always moments like this to look forward to. It was just as I had imagined!

In the end, my journey to the land of Cheesy-La had been a **GREAT** one! What other cavemouse can say he helped discover a long-lost land? You can bet your whiskers I'll be ready for my next adventure in the Stone Age, or I'm not . . .

Geronimo Stiltonoot, cavemouse!

WANT TO READ THE NEXT ADVENTURE OF THE CAVEMICE? I CAN'T WAIT TO TELL YOU ALL ABOUT IT!

THE FAST AND THE FROZEN

A visiting rodent has arrived in Old Mouse City with astounding news. On his recent journey to a cold, distant land, he spotted a mountain . . . moving! Holey cheese! Geronimo Stiltonoot is determined to travel to the ice and snow himself to find out what lies behind this mysterious activity. It's a fur-raising expedition!

Don't miss any of my fabumouse adventures!

#1 Lost Treasure of the Emerald Eye

#2 The Curse of the Cheese Pyramid

#3 Cat and Mouse in a Haunted House

#4 I'm Too Fond of My Fur!

#5 Four Mice Deep in the Jungle

#6 Paws Off, Cheddarface!

#7 Red Pizzas for a Blue Count

#8 Attack of the Bandit Cats

#9 A Fabumouse Vacation for Geronimo

#10 All Because of a Cup of Coffee

#11 It's Halloween, You 'Fraidy Mouse!

#12 Merry Christmas, Geronimo!

#13 The Phantom of the Subway

#14 The Temple of the Ruby of Fire

#15 The Mona Mousa Code

#16 A Cheese-Colored Camper

#17 Watch Your Whiskers, Stilton!

#18 Shipwreck on the Pirate Islands

#19 My Name Is Stilton, Geronimo Stilton

#20 Surf's Up, Geronimo!

#21 The Wild, Wild West

#22 The Secret of Cacklefur Castle

A Christmas Tale

#23 Valentine's Day Disaster

#24 Field Trip to Niagara Falls

#25 The Search for Sunken Treasure

#26 The Mummy with No Name

#27 The Christmas Toy Factory

#28 Wedding Crasher

#29 Down and Out Down Under

#30 The Mouse Island Marathon

#31 The Mysterious Cheese Thief

Christmas Catastrophe

#32 Valley of the Giant Skeletons

#33 Geronimo and the Gold Medal Mystery

#34 Geronimo Stilton, Secret Agent

#35 A Very Merry Christmas

#36 Geronimo's Valentine

#37 The Race Across America

#38 A Fabumouse School Adventure

#39 Singing Sensation

#40 The Karate Mouse

#41 Mighty Mount Kilimanjaro

#42 The Peculiar Pumpkin Thief

#43 I'm Not a Supermouse!

#44 The Giant Diamond Robbery

#45 Save the White Whale!

#46 The Haunted Castle

#47 Run for the Hills, Geronimo!

#48 The Mystery in Venice

#49 The Way of the Samurai

#50 This Hotel is Haunted

#51 The Enormouse Pearl Heist

#52 Mouse in Space!

#53 Rumble in the Jungle

#54 Get into Gear, Stilton!

#55 The Golden Statue Plot

#56 Flight of the Red Bandit

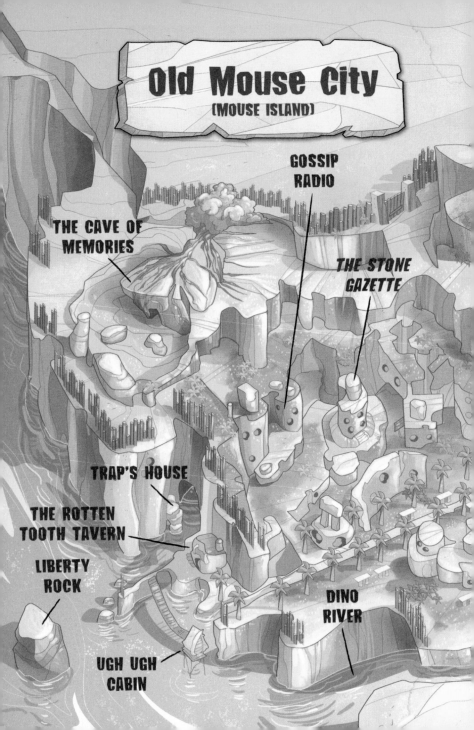

DEAR MOUSE FRIENDS,
THANKS FOR READING,
AND GOOD-BYE UNTIL
THE NEXT BOOK!